The Beast Beneath the Bed

Clemency Pearce

Laura Hughes

BONNEY PRESS

Published by Bonney Press,
an imprint of Hinkler Books Pty Ltd
45–55 Fairchild Street
Heatherton Victoria 3202 Australia
www.hinkler.com.au

BONNEY
PRESS

© Hinkler Books Pty Ltd 2012, 2014

Author: Clemency Pearce
Illustrator: Laura Hughes
Prepress: Graphic Print Group

ISBN: 978 1 7436 3502 5

Printed and bound in China

Each night when warmly snuggled down, when dreams are swirling in my head,

There comes a creepy, crawling noise...

SCRATCH

SCRITCH

...THE BEAST BENEATH THE BED!

The scratchy sounds and little growls echo in the dark.

I pull the covers to my chin and hear him cough and bark.

One day, I snuck a little peek, and saw the fearsome brute.

He was two-feet high, with bright red eyes. Anything but cute!

With tangled fur and awesome fangs, he really was a sight.

His claws were long and razor sharp; he gave me such a fright!

I watched, as he began to steal all my lovely toys.

He ate my smartest pair of shoes, then made a burping noise.

He tore right up the bookcase on lightning little paws.

He chomped on all my fairytales with ferocious snappy jaws.

He swung upon my lampshade,

"WHEEEEEEEEEEEE!",

howling as he flew.

I'd never seen such naughtiness! My horror grew and grew.

Then he fell down,

'BUMP!',

and left a dent upon the floor.

He gobbled up my teddy bear...

...**THAT** was the final straw!

"STOP IT NOW, YOU FIEND!"

I yelled, leaping to my feet.

"You've messed up all my precious things and I like to keep them neat!"

At this the creature froze and stared. He was scared of
me instead!

I found my fear had disappeared of The Beast Beneath The Bed.

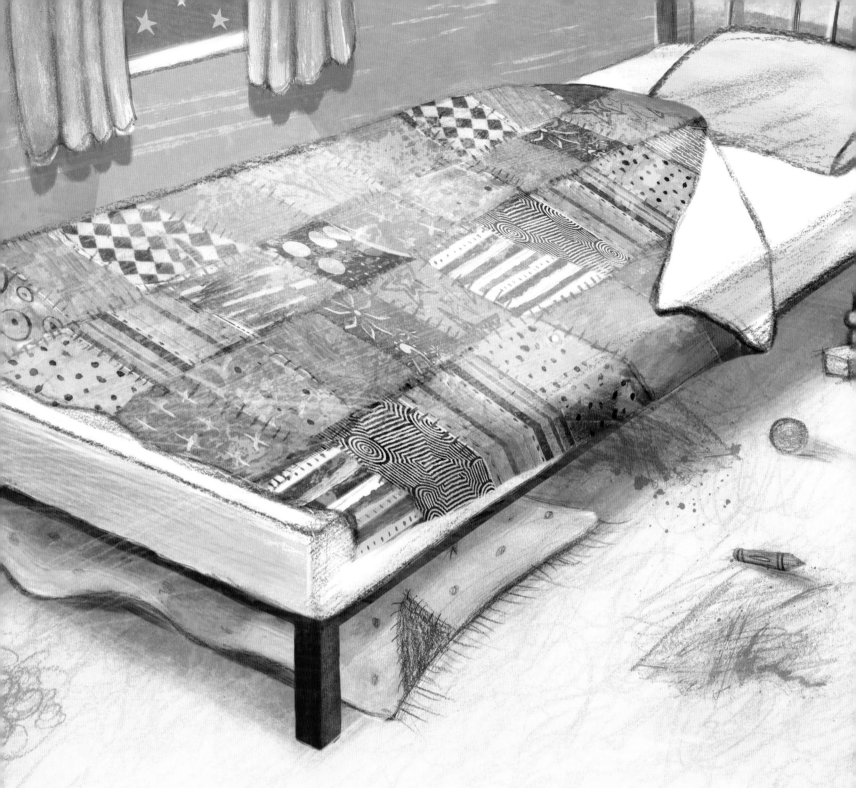

"Why are **YOU** so terrified? So petrified?" I said.

He replied, quite mystified,

"YOU'RE THE BEAST ABOVE MY HEAD!"

"When the sun shines bright and clear, and I'm snoozing in my den,

You ruin all my magic mess by cleaning up again!"

We had both been naughty monsters, in very different ways.

He'd sabotaged my night-times...

and I'd haunted all his days.

So we put our heads together, and we made a special deal.

I'd let him play with all my toys, if he promised not to steal.

He said he wouldn't eat my shoes, if I left him out some bread.

And now there is no talk of beasts; we use proper names instead.

So when I'm drifting off at night, and hear those scratchy snarls,

I just say,

"MORNING, ROBERT!",

and he says,

"GOODNIGHT, CHARLES!"